Sparks Fly

By Aurelia Yates

Copyright © 2023 by Aurelia Yates

All rights reserved.

Visit my website at

https://www.AureliaYatesAuthor.com

Cover Designer: Christy Pierce Photography, LLC

Professional Photographer - Christy Pierce Photography LLC

Editor: https://personaltouchediting.godaddysites.com/

Models: Clint and Lauren Estes-Bailey

https://linktr.ee/laurenestesfit

No part of this book may be reproduced or transmitted in any form or by any means, electronic or mechanical, including photocopying, recording, or by any information storage and retrieval system without the written permission of the author, except for the use of brief quotations in a book review.

This book is a work of fiction. Names, characters, places, and incidents either are products of the author's imagination or are used fictitiously. Any resemblance to actual persons, living or dead, events, or locales is entirely coincidental.

ISBN-: 979-8-9867542-5-3

TABLE OF CONTENTS

Sparks Fly
1

Copyright © 2023 by Aurelia Yates
2

Follow Aurelia on
5

WARNING
6

Chapter One
7

Chapter Two
12

Chapter Three
18

Chapter Four
22

Chapter Five
28

Chapter Six
39

Chapter Seven
42

ABOUT THE AUTHOR
47

Follow Aurelia on

https://www.goodreads.com/author/show/22689072.Aurelia_Yates

https://www.bookbub.com/profile/aurelia-yates

https://www.facebook.com/aureliayatesauthor

https://www.instagram.com/aureliayatesauthor/

https://www.tiktok.com/@aureliayatesauthor

WARRNING

This book is rated R; not appropriate for readers under 18 years of age; contains elements of sex, cheating, and language.

CHAPTER ONE
Maggie

Maggie

Today marks the six month anniversary with my boyfriend—Charles. Our relationship was a dream when we first started dating, but now he acts like I'm not even in the room. Tonight, I plan on pulling out the big guns because Charles is staying over, and I have plans to make him scream!

Slipping my favorite black lace bodice over my head, I let the chiffon skirt flow to where it brushes the top of my thighs. I inspect myself in the mirror, loving how I look in the teddy.

My nipples show through the thin lace top, barely covering my oversized breast, and the soft chiffon skirt floats whimsically around me. I whirl around, admiring my ass and how amazing it looks in the thong with lace matching the bodice.

Charles won't be able to turn me down tonight. I've

been plucked, waxed, and shaved, ready to be devoured.

I step out of the bathroom, stopping at the doorway. Seductively sliding my arm up the door frame, I pose, hoping Charles will shoot his eyes up from his laptop, throw it to the side, and charge at me like a horny bull.

Sadly, that's not the case. So, I clear my throat to get his attention, but nothing, not even a glance.

Walking provocatively, I place one foot in front of the other, causing my hips to sway. When I reach the end of the bed, I crawl up like a cat on the prowl—stopping when I'm nestled between Charles' legs. I peer over his computer at him.

Charles just made editor at the publishing company he works for. I'm so happy for him, but it's sucked the sex and fun out of our relationship, when there was barely any to begin with. I think he cares more about his job than he does about me.

I'm not giving up just yet because Charles is the most responsible man I've been with. Other men I've dated before him have acted like children, and I'm done babysitting.

"Charles," I say in a sexy tone.

"Hmm?" he remarks, not bothering to look up.

I run my hands up his thighs, not stopping till I reach his cock.

"Babe, not now. I have to finish this project."

I blow out a puff of air. Turned down again.

I pull my hand back from his limp dick and sit on my heels. Studying his face, I grow more flustered.

What the hell!

I have never worked as hard to grab his attention as I did today.

Rolling off the bed, I reach into my nightstand and pull out my vibrator.

Fuck this shit. I'm going to get off ... one way or another.

Stomping to the bathroom, I slam the door close. I leave it unlocked because what's the point? It's not like he'll be coming in here demanding I don't use a man-made dick. Any other man would have a fit if their woman used a vibrator, but not Charles. He doesn't have enough masculinity to find it offensive that his woman has to use one to get themselves off.

Turning on the vibrator, I apply the purple rounded end to my clit and run it down my sex, guiding it back up over my clit. I circle the vibrating wand and my insides tighten.

It feels so good.

I don't even care when I scream as my chest heaves from the orgasm I just gave myself.

Leaning against the wall, thoughts of not feeling desire from Charles run rapidly through my mind.

Could he be seeing someone else?

No ... Charles isn't the type to cheat, not the guy you can't trust. Charles is more of a nerd than anything.

His light brown hair sets off his dark brown eyes. He's lean because he runs every day. He doesn't have bulging muscles, but I'm okay with that. I fell for his nerdiness.

I remember the first time I saw him. He was sitting in a corner booth, reading a book while I had lunch with my co-workers. Thinking he was so cute and boyish, I asked the hostess to sit us close to him, hoping to get a chance to talk to him. The opportunity presented itself, and we've been seeing each other ever since.

Maybe, the problem is I've taken control of this relationship and have from the start. It seems like everything we do together, I've always initiated it. I've been the one who has suggested we go hiking, running together in the park, or going to the bookstore, all the things he loves to do.

He's never really shown interest in getting to know me or asked me where I would like to go on date night.

The sex has always been on the vanilla side, but at least we had a sex life—unlike now. I use the word 'had' loosely because it's been dry the last month, maybe two. It's not only the sex—it's everything. He's distanced himself. Every relationship hits a rock, or perhaps it's time for me to end this.

I wash up and change into my *Wonder Woman* nightshirt because, unlike me, she would know how to handle this situation.

Defeated, I walk out of the bathroom with my shoulders slumped. I slide my friend back into the nightstand drawer, then slip under the covers.

Charles doesn't speak. I wonder if he heard me when I screamed out my release.

If he did, would he care?

Lying on my back, I look up at the ceiling. I've been doing this a lot lately, staring into the empty white space above the bed, waiting for something to happen between us, waiting for something to change for us to become closer.

I let myself gaze at the white ceiling tiles for half an hour. Charles closes his laptop and sets it on the nightstand with his glasses. Turning the light off, he lies on his back.

"My mom invited us up to the lake house for the Fourth of July weekend," Charles says nonchalantly.

My eyes almost budge out. He's never introduced me to his family. I only know bits and pieces about his family.

I get a little giddy when I speak. "You want to introduce me to your mom and stepdad?"

I can't see very well in the dark, but I think he just shrugged his shoulder.

"My stepbrother will be there, and I'm sure he'll bring a plus one, so I thought I would ask you to come."

He only asked me because he fears his brother showing him up—the nerve to even say that out loud.

I don't respond. Instead, I imagine pressing my pillow over his face and smothering the life out of him.

CHAPTER TWO
Maggie

Maggie

The following morning, when I wake up, Charles is gone. Thank goodness I don't feel like seeing him. I'm still upset he left me to care for my libido. Then there's the invitation to his parents' lake house. Did he invite me to be with him or ask me to have a plus one?

I didn't even know Charles had a stepbrother. He never talks about his family. If it wasn't for the single portrait of his mom and stepdad in his living room, I would have thought he was an orphan.

Lying in bed a few moments longer than I should, my mind won't stop contemplating if I should break it off before the Fourth of July or if I should go to see if I win over his parents, if I might win Charles back.

I decide to give our relationship another chance because I want this to work out. I'm not a quitter. I make goals and accomplish them.

I spring into action for the day. I need to buy a new bathing suit that will hopefully make Charles think of sex when he sees me in something that shows off the goods.

I dial Macy's number. Macy has been my best friend since I moved to Charlotte a few years ago. One day in the breakroom, we shared our hatred for our cunt of a boss, which caused an instant bond between us. Macy is a true romantic. She's always doing thoughtful exclamations of showing her boyfriend how much she loves him. That's why she is my go to person in trying to keep Charles's interest in me alive.

My parents live in a rural area, but I love the hustle and bustle of city life. Maybe, one day, when I have children, I'll move to the quiet rural area where my sister and I grew up.

"I have something to tell you," Macy says, excitement oozing out.

"What is it?" I ask, eager to hear what she will say.

"Joel asked me to marry him last night!" she shouts into the phone.

"Oh, Macy, I'm so excited for you." I do my best to sound excited, but I'm afraid it doesn't come out too cheerful.

I'm truly happy for Macy, but a small part is jealous.

I never thought I would be twenty-eight and still not hitched. Judging by how Charles and I are going, I may be single for the rest of my life.

We discuss her plans for the wedding and how she wants to marry in the spring of next year. Then we make plans for me to swing by her apartment, pick her up, and head to the nearest shop so I can buy a bathing suit.

Grabbing my small designer bag, I casually walk out of my front door and lock it. When I reach the elevator, I press the down arrow and patiently wait.

Using the downtime, I pull out my cell and scroll through my social media. Post after post, I see all my friends with their significant others. They look so happy together. Feelings of being alone for the rest of my life play out in my mind. Will Charles and I ever look like that? Is he worth all the work I put into this relationship?

Hearing the elevator doors open, I step into it. Still staring at the over-sickening photos of happy couples, I walk face-forward into a wall. I look up to see to a six-four wall of muscle with the gorgeous face of a Greek god, amused by me being pressed against him. His lips turn up on one side, and his eyes draw me in. They're a breathtaking gray with specks of blue. I'm barely able to speak.

"So sorry," I stutter.

He smells so good! His cologne smells rich and spicey. His hair is still damp, I'm guessing from a shower. Realizing I'm still pressed up against him. I quickly peel myself away. He feels so good. Solid and robust, everything Charles isn't.

He chuckles, wraps his arms around me, pulling me flush to his body, and says in a deep rumble, "I'm not complaining." His eyes look down into the V-neck of my shirt. Licking his lips, he says, "Those tits would look better in my mouth with you on my cock."

Heat floods my face. I feel the embarrassment of the red splotches creeping up from my neck to my cheeks.

The dirty talking man sends tingles leading straight to my sex. My chest rises and falls in a hard rhythm. Stunned by his provocative words, I'm speechless and turned on.

His broad smile tells me he's having fun at my expense.

I wiggle out of his embrace when the car doors open. Bolting out of the elevator, I sprint to my vehicle, trying not to be concerned when I hear the deep chuckle that echoes through the parking deck.

Making it to my car, I jump in, trying to hide behind the steering wheel as I watch him. His walk is slow, and fuck, he looks perfect in those dark denim jeans hanging from his waist and snugging his perfect ass.

He stops at a motorcycle parked one row from me. When he lifts his arms to put on his helmet, I notice how his muscles flex.

God, he's big.

When he straddles the seat, I imagine him naked, standing behind me, ready to push himself inside me.

What am I thinking? I have a boyfriend!

I've been sex-deprived for way too long.

He starts the bike, and with his large hands on the handles, he revs the engine.

God, he looks so good on that bike. I can imagine the power he holds between his legs.

I take several quick breaths when he speeds off to calm my hormones. Suddenly, I wish I was on the bike naked, legs spread, waiting for him to ride me.

Finally, I start my car and exit the parking garage, headed to pick up Macy. The entire drive, my mind goes wild, thinking of the different sexual positions I would love to try on that motorcycle—with him.

Twenty minutes later, I pull into the parking lot at Macy's building.

Macy opens the door and squeals, showing off the two-carat pear-shaped rock on her finger.

The smile on my face spreads to my heart. I'm so excited my friend is about to marry the man she has loved for so long. To share the joy of her engagement fills me with contentment. I'm pleased to see the happiness she expresses on her face and body language.

We laugh all the way from Macy's complex until we enter the department store. Dillan's has a massive selection of the latest styles in bathing suits, so I know I will find something from their large floor display.

As we search through the rack of bikinis, I tell Macy how things have been with Charles for the past few months. She gives me a sympathetic look, and it makes me want to crawl into a hole. The last thing I want from anyone is that look. It's bad enough I feel sorry for myself. I don't need my best friend to take pity on me.

"Why are you going? You need to let him go," Macy pleads.

Macy has never liked Charles. Maybe she saw something from the beginning that I didn't.

"I owe it to myself to give this one more chance."

Am I trying to convince her or myself?

Before she can remark, I see what could be the sexiest, tiniest swimsuit.

"This is it!" I cheer as I hold up a strappy black leather bikini.

Her jaw drops. "Now that is sexy!" she says with a

purr.

I run the suit through my hand, feeling the leather's softness. The bottoms are a cheeky cut, and the small triangles covering the breasts are small and thin. It's perfect.

"This will turn his head," I say with confidence.

"If he sees you in that and doesn't get hard for you, you need to drop his ass," Macy says.

CHAPTER THREE
Maggie

Maggie

Charles and I rode the entire hour and a half to the lake house in comfortable silence. When we pull up in front of a white three-story home with large surrounding wraparound windows that would give the perfect view of the lake from any angle inside the house, I can't help but gasp.

It's breathtaking and looks so serene. They have docked a large platoon boat along with two wave runners. The boat ramp, is close to a large, covered porch, with patio lounge chairs facing an infinity pool.

"It's stunning," I murmur.

Charles barely looks up at it. "Yeah, it's nice."

I knew his family had money, but I didn't realize they had this much money. Charles can be a snob, and now I can see why. He's used to having the finer things.

My parents were and are lower-middle class. We

didn't have much when I grew up. I had to take out mounds of student loans because my parents couldn't afford to pay for my college, but it was worth it. As a certified public accountant, I've established a good-paying job and a grand apartment.

"Maggie," Charles has his hand placed on my shoulder, shaking me just a little.

"Oh, sorry."

"Let's get the luggage so we can get settled. Mom and Connor are waiting on us," he tells me while he unbuckles his seatbelt.

We get out of the car and grab the luggage from the trunk.

As I roll my suitcase into the garage to enter the home, I have a feeling this weekend is going to be an adventure.

***

I wake up as usual at six o'clock. Getting up early has always been in me. My internal alarm clock won't allow me to sleep late.

Gathering my bathing suit out of my bag. I head into the en suite bath to dress and pull my hair up.

Charles' mother placed him in a bedroom on the opposite side of the house. I don't think his mother likes me very much. When Charles introduced me to his parents, his stepdad was friendly, pulling me into a warm hug and giving me a gentle smile as he greeted me. However, his mom ... well, let's just say she didn't move a muscle from her stance. The only thing that showed any life was her lip when it curled upward into a sneer. It took all I had to refrain from slapping that smugness from her perfectly red painted Botox injected lips.

She did her best not to speak to me last night at dinner. I tried to make conversation, but she would cut me off when I tried to speak. Also, the way his mother babysat him at the table was off the charts crazy, but what was more bizarre was how he responded. I think he was on his mother's tit too long when he was breastfed.

I shrug it off. Today is a new day. I plan on lying by the pool, putting this new bathing suit to the test to get Charles standing at attention.

Sliding the last bobby pin in my hair, I grab my sunglasses and towel, then slide on my flip-flops.

Walking down the hall to Charles' room, I tiptoe softly past his parents' room, trying to be quiet. I don't want to wake the beast. When I get to Charles's room, he's not there, so I proceed to the kitchen.

When I see Charles, I notice a beautiful brunette sitting in the kitchen nook with him. She looks to be in her early twenties with long brown hair and a small frame. He's looking at her longingly, laughing at something she just said.

He seems to be in a dream state as his eyes scan her features, making my heart drop and my body go cold. A small amount of jealousy creeps in that he's never looked at me like that. That look, the one that says I'll do anything for this person.

Maybe it's his sister? He's never mentioned a sister, but he never mentioned he had a stepbrother, either.

I square my shoulders to speak, but when Charles spots me, his face falls, and the beautiful smile collapses. His eyes shift from me to the brunette as if I had caught his hand in the cookie jar.

A moment passes. I wait for him to introduce me,

but he doesn't speak.

"Hi, I'm Nat," the young, perky girl says.

"Hello, I'm Maggie."

"I live next door." Nat points out the window to the blue house, which is larger than Charles's parents.

"I just came over to tell Charles hello. We grew up together. Well, I was several years younger." She giggles.

"I'm headed to the pool. Do you care to join me?" I ask Charles, but I look at Nat as well. I don't want to be rude, but the thought of having to watch my boyfriend make goo-goo eyes at her makes my stomach turn into a knot.

"In a bit," Charles says with a tight lip.

I nod and smile, feeling like a fool.

Maybe I'll ask him to take me home since it's apparent he doesn't want me here, not with the way he was giving her his full attention.

Grabbing a bottle of water from the small refrigerator under the kitchen cabinet, I look out at the oasis waiting for me to sunbathe in.

I strut to a lounge chair beside the pool and spread my towel over the chair, spitting out a few unkind words about Charles and what an ass he is.

While I soak in the sun, my eyes close, as the warm rays heat my skin. I wonder if I made the right choice coming this weekend.

CHAPTER FOUR
Colt

Colt

Standing to the side of the house, I hang my matte black Beanie helmet on the handlebars of my Harley. I just arrived at my dad and stepmother's lake house.

I wasn't coming this weekend, and if it wasn't for my dad sounding disappointed when I told him I needed to work, I wouldn't be here.

The bar I own was a complete dive when I bought it, but I've turned it back into its glory state. It's slowly becoming a popular site with the locals and even the surrounding towns.

You would think my stepmother would give me recognition. I've done everything on my own at the young age of twenty-two, but my stepmother's snooty ways think a bar is beneath her. Her demands of always wanting to be in high society's social life, only eating at five-star restaurants, being at fancy country clubs, and socializing with people who care less about her have never interested me. Her son possesses many of her snooty traits.

Running my hands through my short, dark hair, the sound of someone spitting out profanity catches my attention.

I spot a set of gorgeous long, toned, and tanned legs. My eyes move up to a perfect, tight ass that makes my dick twitch, but when I scan her breast and her barely covered tits, my cock hardens.

Fuck!

Seeing her face, I realize it's the girl from my apartment complex. Her blonde hair is up into a messy bun, displaying more of her tan skin around her slender neck.

My dick hardens to full mast, pushing against my zipper, and begging to be released.

I can still feel how it felt to have her pushed against me.

Who the hell is she? Why is she here?

I adjust my cock.

Fuck, she's hot!

Walking out onto the back patio, I stand over her, blocking the sun. I use this moment to get a close look at her full lips and think about how badly I want to see parted as she screams while I pound into her.

Her head stretches up, trying to look up at me. She lets out a small gasp through her plump lips.

"Umm, can I help you?" Her voice comes out shaky.

She can help me with this rod in my pants.

"I'm Colt," I announce, "And you are?"

"Maggie," she whispers.

"Don't I know you?" Pulling my t-shirt over my head, I don't miss how her lips part and her nipples harden through the thin leather fabric. She has sunglasses on, but I can tell she's enjoying the view. I see her throat work.

"I'm not sure. Can you move? You're blocking the sun."

"Are you sure?" I grin. "You can admit if you would rather—"

"I would rather have the sun burn my eyes out." She makes a swiping motion with her hand.

A smirk creeps up on my face. Feisty as shit is just my type. Moving to the lounge chair beside her, I throw my shirt down and unzip my pants.

"What are you doing?

"I'm taking off my pants." I give her a cocky grin.

"I can see that. Why?" she asks as her face reddens.

I point to the pool. "I'm going to take a swim."

My pants slide down my legs. She's facing forward, but I can tell she's watching. The slight tilt in her head gives her away. Facing her, I allow her to have a full view of the outline of my cock. Wanting her to get an idea of what I could offer her to pleasure her with. She twists her head, looking in the opposite direction. I can't help the little chuckle that escapes my lips.

Strolling to the side of the pool, aware of lingering eyes roaming my backside, I turn to confirm my suspicion, and right away, I'm met with Maggie's eyes peering up at me as I dive into the pool. The cool water instantly sends a refreshing sensation through my body.

I swim over to the corner, closer to Maggie. Putting my arms on the concrete edge and propping my chin on my hands, I admire her soft curves. My hands itch to explore them, to hold her tight in my arms while I pinch her nipples until they hurt.

Maggie pulls her sunglasses down. I love the way her green eyes sparkle. "What are you doing?" she says, almost in a whisper.

"I'm thinking about how good you would look with my head buried between your thighs."

Her body reacts to my words by pressing her legs together. I want to pry them apart and spread them wide to get a view of her pussy.

Her mouth opens to say something, but Charles comes out of the house with a deep frown plastered on his face. I roll my eyes. This guy is a buzz kill.

"I wasn't sure if you would show up. Where's your date?" Charles spits out.

Charles has always had a dislike for me, much like his mother. My mother died when I was young, and my dad married his mother a year after my mom's death. I know the marriage was to fill in the gap of my mom, but Connie has never treated me like a son.

"Came alone," I tell him without moving my eyes from the beautiful woman in the lounge chair.

Charles makes a move to walk over to Maggie, but doesn't take his eyes off me. "This is my girlfriend, Maggie."

Not for long.

Maggie is way too hot for him. It might be the asshole coming out, but I doubt Maggie will leave with him once our little vacation ends.

Nat walks out of the kitchen onto the patio. "Colt!" she yells excitedly, letting the smile spread wide on her face.

"Hey, you!" I jump out of the pool to give her a hug. Thank God, my hard erection has come down. Wrapping my arms around Nat, I notice how Charles looks like he's about to bust. He's always had a thing for her.

"You're getting me wet," Nat says with a hint of seduction.

Nat and her family purchased the beach house next door at the same time my dad bought this one. We all grew up together, and even though Nat has always had a crush on me, I've never seen her as anything but a sister.

"I thought your family was spending the summer in Europe," I ask Nat.

"I didn't go. I just wanted to keep tradition and be here."

Throwing my arm around her shoulders, I say, with a devilish smile, "I know I'm not the only one that's happy to see you." I glance in Charles's direction and instantly get pleasure from the sour expansion on his face. Fucking with Charles over Nat has always run high on my to-do list.

My eyes find Maggie flinching at my words, shrinking into herself while pushing her sunglasses further up the bridge of her nose. *Fuck!* I wasn't even thinking about how my words would hurt her. I instantly feel like an ass.

Seeing Maggie shrink into herself like a child who's been disciplined causes me pain in my chest. I usually don't give a fuck about hurting any woman. The women who surround me are fast, easy, and come back for another second helping of being treated like shit. Maggie, she's not that type. She's a woman that deserves to be treated like a princess, something that Charles doesn't know how to treat any woman other than himself, the pussy.

I've never had a girlfriend, never taken a girl out on an actual date. Only hookups with no sparks have held my interest, but I feel something tug at me, noticing the hurt on Maggie's face.

CHAPTER FIVE
Maggie

Maggie

I have never felt so out of place as I do at this very moment. The way Colt teased Charles about not being the only one who was happy to see Nat has left a hole in my chest. I couldn't tell anyone the last time Charles was excited to see me walk into a room.

Charles didn't even give me a side-eye when he said I was his girlfriend. It just seemed like he said it to establish ownership.

What an ass!

I can't believe I've never seen Colt in my or our apartment complex. He's definitely someone you would have noticed before. Maybe he doesn't live there but was just visiting someone.

I couldn't own up to the fact that, yes, it was me who ran straight into his chest. I was way too embarrassed about what had happened. Only a ditzy girl does such things. So, I did my best to play it cool and pretend I didn't know him. When, really, he was all I could think about at night. His arms wrapped around me, pressing his body into his, and how he talked so dirty, leaving a pool of wetness in my panties. He consumes my mind, even in my dreams.

Charles's stepdad, Connor, comes out of the house.

"Maggie, did you have a good night's sleep?"

I smile. "Yes, sir." Charles's stepdad is a pleasure to be around.

I don't know why he married the troll.

"Colt!" Connor yells excitedly, walking over to greet his son and taking him into a hug.

They are the same height and build, with strong facial features. Good looks run deep in their genes. Both with dark hair, except Connor's has a little salt mixed in. They make Charles look like a charity case.

Charles has too much of his mother in him. His eyes are small and round, and his top lip has no shape. He's only five-nine feet with a slender build.

Connor pats Colt on the back, and I can see the sparkle in Connor's eye when he looks at his son.

"Let's take the boat out after lunch," Connor says with an enormous grin, looking at his son.

Charles mutters under his breath, but when Nat cheers, jumping up and down, making her small chest bounce with each movement, Charles grins, staring at them.

I look down at my full breasts. My girls resemble a small Volkswagen in a bathtub. There's just no room! Nat's chest is so tiny that it would hardly fit into a bathroom sink, let alone a bathtub.

I guess small tits do it for him.

When I tilt my head back up, I meet Colt's eyes. He

gives me a wink, making butterflies erupt in my stomach.

My God, I can't be having butterflies for Charles's stepbrother. How wrong is that?

I couldn't stop thinking about him before, but now that I know he's Charles's stepbrother, I can't look at the forbidden fruit, much less take a bite—although a bite wouldn't hurt me. It's not like Charles has offered me some of his fruits lately.

No, Maggie, stop thinking about Colt's nuts.

After the discussion of taking the boat out, everyone gathers outside, enjoying the morning. Charles's mother and I are sitting in the chairs, watching the volleyball game in the pool between Charles and Nat versus Connor and Colt.

I've not been able to take my eyes off Colt, loving how his body moves and his muscles stretch. It's truly amazing how he moves with ease. I've tried my best not to drool, but this heat is not making it easy.

When it's Colt's turn to serve the ball, he stands straighter, and when he throws the ball in the air, I moan a little. My eyes focus on his muscles flexing and the water dripping from his perfect physique. When he hits the ball, I'm too dazed when I realize the ball is heading my way. I let out a scream when it hits me square in the face. Damn it, that hurt!

"Shit, Maggie," Colt jumps out of the water and runs over. "You're bleeding. Let me help you."

"I'll take care of her," Charles demands.

Charles stands back from me, looking pale. About as much help as a panty liner on a heavy flow day while on my period. Colt doesn't pay him any attention. He keeps trying to help me. My frustration grows at Charles for being a wimp at the sight of a little blood.

"I can take care of myself," I say as I grab my towel and hold it to my nose.

Jumping up and almost running into the house, I go into the powder room, shutting the door behind me. There's a small knock. When the door opens slowly, Colt pops his head in.

"I'm coming in," he announces, walking in without asking.

I want to say no because I don't know if I can control my hormones. Being in a tiny space with a half-naked Colt is more than I can handle.

He approaches me with caution, remorse written on his face.

"Let me." He takes the towel from me.

Turning the faucet on, he wets the corner of the towel. Bringing it to my face, he slides his hand up to cup my head while he wipes under my nose.

"Hold still. I can't concentrate with your breasts bouncing around."

"Ouch," I cry out as Colt presses a little too hard. "Stop looking at my breasts. They're not the object that's hurting."

"I bet I could suck and tease them into a painful state." He raises a cocky eyebrow, waiting for an invitation.

"Focus on the true task, my nose and not my breasts."

"I didn't mean to hit you in the nose."

I look up at him.

"I was planning on it passing you, but my aim was off."

"Why would you do that?"

We look into each other's eyes. "I wanted your eyes on me."

I'm overcome with numbness. The thought of this gorgeous man wanting my eyes on him when he can seek someone so much younger, like Nat. My blood rushing to parts of my body, and I immediately know it's wrong. There is the overwhelming feeling of lust, but I can't help it. I want Colt to devour me, consume me whole. There is this insatiable need inside of me I need filling, and he is the only one that can fill it.

He's too young. He's Charles's stepbrother, but when his eyes keep flicking between my lips and eyes, I can't help but want to taste him.

He slowly stops wiping my nose. Drawing the towel to his side. He discards it on the basin and then wraps his hand behind my head. Tilting my head back, he leans in and brushes his lips against mine. It's a soft, wet, passionate kiss that creates sparks on my lips. The tingles run through my body, leaving me wanting more.

We stand in the middle of the bathroom, our lips and tongues dancing together. My hands have made their way into his hair, tugging and pulling him into me. When I pull back, I'm breathless.

I see my reflection in the mirror, and guilt races in my mind. Why did I do that?

"I can't. I ... I shouldn't have kissed you." I draw away, trying to put distance between us.

When I try to walk past Colt, he grabs my hand.

"You can't tell me you didn't feel that." He pauses. "Your body tells me you did and want it just as much as I do."

I look at the door, wanting to escape this reality because he's right. I felt it, and I want more—more of his tongue and lips on my body.

There are just a few problems. He's so much younger than me, and he's Charles's stepbrother.

This thing between Charles and me is clearly not working, but I need someone who I feel certain is not using me to make their brother jealous. I need someone who is older than Colt. God! He's only twenty-two. I'm twenty-eight. I'm ready to settle down. He probably still wants to play around.

I won't deny my attraction to Colt ... can't deny it. He's beautiful.

I could see being with him, but not now, knowing that he's related to Charles, knowing he's so much younger than me. I mean, really, how stable could he be?

Pulling my hand out of his embrace, I leave him watching me as I exit the powder room.

***

Ever since I walked out of the bathroom, leaving Colt alone, I've tried not to think about him. I've done my best not to make eye contact, but he sits next to me and brushes against me.

Lunch is amazing. Charles' mother has sub sandwiches with all the trimmings laid out in a beautiful spread. I try to give the old bat a compliment, but she just grunts. She's slick. She gives me a smile when other people are around, but when no one else is around, she shows her true colors.

Everyone is boarding the pontoon boat. Charles is walking in front of me, and I'm the caboose ... well, actually, Colt is.

The dock is the only thing I can see that needs a little repair, but I'm guessing it's from the weather. Stubbing my toes on the bow-up board causes me to drop my bag. When I bend over to pick it up, I feel hands on my hips and something hard pressed against my ass.

"Do you need help?" Colt says as his fingers dig into my hips.

Fuck me.

Closing my eyes, I take a deep gulp of air. This is by far the hottest vacation I've ever had.

I rise, pushing Colt's hands from my hips. "I've got it," I say, looking around to see if anyone noticed Colt's hard and impressive cock pressed into my ass.

I make my way to the waiting crowd on the boat. As far as I can tell, not one person looks in our direction. I get the impression his stepmother cares as much for him as she does for me.

Once we are all loaded on the elegant oversized ride, Colt pushes the boat from the dock and comes to sit across from me. The grin he gives me leaves me antsy in my seat.

Fifteen minutes later, Connor stops the boat.

"Colt, get the float, Big Bertha, out, and you guys can take turns riding," Colt's dad says.

After they blow the float up, they toss it into the lake.

"Maggie, ride the float," Connor says.

"I don't think I should." I plead.

Colt gives me a sinful grin, and my intuition tells me I'm not about to like what he's going to do. So, I try to prepare to make a run for it.

Where in the hell can I go? I'm on a boat in the middle of a lake.

When Colt lunges for me, I scream as he flips me over his shoulder and jumps off the side, causing us to bounce off the float when we land.

When we go under, I can feel Colt's hand slide up from my leg, squeezing my ass. When we come up for air, I swat his shoulder.

He gives me a smile, and I can't help but return it.

We're a few feet away from the large boat where his family is waiting for us to climb onto the float. Once I'm on top of Big Bertha, I wait for Colt to join me.

He pulls himself up, taking the same position, both of us on our stomachs. When he gets into position, he places his long, powerful frame up against me.

"Safety first," he says with a cocky smirk.

With an arm stretched over me, he signals to his dad to start the boat. The movement of the float is slow at first, but his dad picks up speed. The float jumps and lands hard on the water's surface. My chest plants roughly onto the float. Each time we jump in the air, my chest bounces more.

"Fuck, your tits are amazing."

What the hell!

I don't know what he's saying until the small leather strap from my bikini flies up and hits me in the eye, causing me to peer down at my boobs. My top has completely come off my boobs, and my girls are free as they bounce with each hard hit.

"Oh, shit!"

I knew this was a bad idea.

"I could watch your tits bounce all night," Colt says in my ear.

I need to get my top tied, but I can't let go, or I'll go

flying into the water backward, giving everyone a show.

The next hard wave sends the float so high, we are about to dive into the water headfirst.

Like I could be so lucky!

Letting a scream out, I feel Colt press up against me closer. I do my best to stay still because, for one, my top is no longer securely tied, and for another, his closeness has me squirming, trying to put pressure on my clit.

When I flex my hips again, applying more pressure, Colt notices.

"Don't worry, I'll take care of that for you," Colt husky voice says as he snakes his hand between my thighs.

I turn my head to look at him. "How is your hand on my thigh supposed to help?"

"Tell me you don't want my hand on that perfect pussy."

His dirty words make me weak. I can't form words to tell him this shouldn't happen.

"Baby." His tongue licks my neck. "Just imagine it's my cock buried inside you."

I suck in a breath when Colt licks the drops of water from my shoulder.

"Colt ... stop ... don't," I say breathlessly, feeling the dampness pooling between my thighs.

"Are you sure you want me to stop?"

Am I sure?

I'm not sure of anything right now. I can't think. I can't move. Hell, I don't know how I got myself into this mess. I'm topless on a damn death trap with a hot-as-fuck guy with his hand between my thighs. I'm going straight to hell.

Colt's finger eases into the elastic band of my bottoms as he moves it up and down my pussy. I moan, reveling in Colt's soft touch. I should tell him no and push him off this death wish we are on, but all I feel right now, at this very moment, is how badly I want his hand to touch me.

Colt's lips touch my ear. "Spread your legs for me."

"Somebody's going to see us." I panic a little inside, wanting to push his hand away but afraid to let go of Big Bertha.

"No one is paying us any attention. Come on baby, spread those gorgeous legs open for me," Colt says as he kisses my ear.

Yep, I'm going straight to hell.

As I push my left leg out, we hit a wave, making the float fly up in the air. When the float slams back down, it hits the water with significant force. Colt's finger thrust into me, and a scream burst out that the gods above could hear.

Holy fuck! That feels so amazing.

When we bolt up again out of the water, hovering over the float for a moment, Colt pushes another finger in, causing me to scream again. With every wave we hit, my clit gets a jolt of electricity as Colt works his fingers inside me. Using his index finger, he strokes my clit. My eyes roll back, and my grip is so tight on the woven handles, they are about to unravel.

"That's it, baby. Scream my name when you come." Colt bites my neck. "I want to feel that tight, sweet pussy squeezing my fingers."

It only takes one more thrust, one more crashing down on the water before I'm screaming Colt's name as the most unbelievable pleasure I've ever had races through my body, making me tremble and turning me into a weak mess. Colt pulls his hand out of my swim bottoms, placing it around my waist.

I raise my head and meet his dad's eyes.

Fuck! Did his dad see us? See Colt finger me?

"I've got you. Let go of the handles." Colt tells me, pulling me from the fear that's washing over me like shame.

When I unclench my hands from the woven bars, we fall off the raft into the water. Colt's arms securely wrap around me as we resurface, shielding my breasts from prying eyes.

Blinking, reality sets in. I'm unsure what to say. Awareness of my betrayal of Charles seeps into the deepest place of my mind. I'm upset at myself for allowing Colt to touch me.

CHAPTER SIX
Colt

Colt

Maggie has fear written on her face, and I can tell she wants to run from me, but I won't let her. I want all her screams. I want all her pleasure to be at my hands, my cock, and my tongue. I have to show her Charles is not the man she's supposed to be with.

"Maggie, look at me," I demand, using a stern voice.

"Stop. I can't believe I just let you do that." She runs her hands down her face. "Charles is your brother and my boyfriend. I shouldn't have done that."

"He's my stepbrother," I bite out. "Who's a fucking moron for not giving you the attention you deserve," I tell Maggie honestly.

Her eyes cast down, and her face goes pale. I'm not sure if it's the words I just threw out at her or if it's the fact that she feels guilty about what we just did. Regardless of what it is, I want to tell her she deserves more than Charles.

"Let me help you with your top."

She slaps my hand as she tries to grab the strings floating around her in the water.

"I can't believe I did that," she mutters, battling with herself.

When Maggie gets her top tied, I see my dad has turned around, making his way back to pick us up. When he gets close, he yells, "We hadn't even noticed you guys fell off!" He laughs.

"No worries," I tell my dad.

"See, I told you no one was paying us any attention," I whisper to Maggie.

Maggie has a blank expression on her face, and I can't read what she's thinking. I just know I want to hold her, but I'm not able to. I have to keep reminding myself she's not with me. She's with the prick—Charles.

We climb into the boat, exchanging places with Charles and Nat.

Maggie sits on the seat opposite my dad, doing her best to ignore me, and looking everywhere but in my direction.

I want to demand her attention and feel her eyes on my body, but I sit and admire her from the closest seat to her. I know she's battling what just happened between us, but before long, I plan on making it known, she's mine.

My dad winks at me before saying, "You know the annual carnival is tonight, along with the fireworks show at the main campgrounds," he announces, looking between Maggie and me.

Does he know?

My dad's a smart man. He's the chief executive officer of a highly respected construction company, and he has an eye for details. That's how he got to be in his position. If anyone can pick up on this thing between Maggie and me, it would be him.

"I'm down with going," I look at Maggie.

She's looking over the water, not paying anyone any attention.

"Maggie," my dad says.

She doesn't answer.

CHAPTER SEVEN
Maggie

Maggie

I'm so lost in my own thoughts, I barely hear Connor talking.

"Sorry, yeah, sounds good." I give a meek smile.

I should be glowing with satisfaction because that was one hell of an orgasm Colt gave me. Instead, I'm overcome with shame. I allowed Colt to finger fuck me in daylight, on a float, being pulled by his family.

What the hell was I thinking?

Should I confess to Charles what just happened? I shouldn't keep this a secret. *Or can I?*

Thinking hard about it, the part of my brain that's telling me to wait wins. Maybe I'll wait till we get back to the city. Then I won't have to deal with the shit hitting the fan in front of his family.

Laughter comes from behind us. When I turn around to see Charles and Nat, they exchange smiles and appear cozy with each other.

Charles seems to be more open this weekend since Nat arrived. Unlike the Charles, I deal with. That Charles is a cold, mute asshole.

The boat slows, and I realize we're back at the dock. Everyone gathers their belongings to go get ready for the festivities for tonight.

I'm gathering my sunscreen, towel, and bag when Charles walks up and picks up my bag. The kind gesture alarms me. Without notice, Charles sneezes, spraying my arm with mucus. I scrunch my nose in disgust, wiping myself with my towel.

"I'm not feeling well," Charles whines.

"I think I'm going to stay in my room tonight," Charles lets out another sneeze.

Thankfully, I'm able to dodge it.

Wasn't he just laughing with Nat a few minutes ago?

I look at Charles with suspicion.

"Nat, do you want to go to the carnival?" Colt asks, making my thoughts drift off.

"I may come for a bit. I was planning on working on my SA for my marketing class."

"Are you in college?" I ask.

"Yes, I'm trying to finish this next semester, but I need to pass this class if I want to graduate in the spring," Nat replies.

"Just you and me, Maggie." Colt wiggles his eyebrows, and I feel my cheeks heating.

"I ... I need to stay ... to take care of Charles," I stammer.

"No, you go. Go have fun," Charles insists. "I'll be okay. I'm just going straight to bed."

He's insisting? That's new.

I exhale the breath in my lungs. "I don't want to

leave with you being sick."

"I'm fine," Charles says with irritation.

Without replying, I grab my bag from Charles and head to my room to get ready. If he insists, then I'll just go, and maybe I can get another mind blowing orgasm from Colt. Fuck Charles!

An hour later, I'd had a refreshing shower, got dressed, and threw my shoulder bag over my head. I look at myself in the mirror, and there it is again—guilt—looking at me straight in the face.

I have to tell Charles. I don't think I'll be able to face myself in the mirror again if I don't.

Before I can change my mind, my feet are heading to Charles' bedroom. I turn the handle without knocking, needing to get this off my chest.

Surprise, shock, and relief pass through me. Charles is in bed with Nat naked on top of him, riding him hard. He's holding her hips, grunting and moaning. He never made noises like that with me.

I don't say a word. I can't. Charles opens his eyes, spots me, and has an expression of a deer caught in headlights.

Going to his dresser, I grab the car keys. I hear Charles call my name, but I don't give a shit. Walking to my bedroom, I start throwing my things into my bag.

Charles dashes into my room, stuttering, trying to apologize, but I don't hear him. All I can think about is getting out of here.

I know I have no right to judge Charles for his actions because of what I've done, so I'm doing my best not to reply and stay calm. If I'm truly being honest with myself, I don't love Charles, and a part of me knows he never loved me.

"I'm sorry, Maggie," Charles holds the blanket around his waist. "It just happened. Things haven't been going well between us, and I have needs."

Now I'm pissed. It's not like I haven't tried to have sex with him. He's the one who has been turning me down.

I slap the shirt in my hand into my suitcase, anger building inside me.

"You and I aren't ... well, we aren't on the same level," Charles says.

My head whips up. "What the hell is that supposed to mean?" I bellow. I pick up my suitcase, ready to walk out.

"Well ... I just mean that you come from a different class of people."

I'm completely annoyed with Charles's behavior. Sleeping with Nat doesn't even bother me, but now, when he talks about the class of people I come from, my mouth explodes, and I point my finger at him.

"You entitled snob. You think you're so high and mighty, but really, you have nothing. It's your parents who have this house and nice things. You live in a one-bedroom apartment that's worse than the one I live in." I stand in the doorway with my hand on the handle. "By the way, your stepbrother doesn't mind what kind of class I come from. He finger fucked me on the float, and it was the best damn orgasm I've ever had."

His face falls flat, and satisfaction spreads through me.

I slam the door, not giving a shit how he feels. Colt

is in the hallway and tries to stop me, but I put my hands up.

"No, I need to leave. If only things were different, but they're not." I kiss him on the cheek.

When I walk away from Colt, I hear crashing against the bedroom walls, where I imagine Charles is having a toddler fit.

***

Continue to find out more about Maggie and Colt in
Sparks Ignite.
Coming June 2024

ABOUT THE AUTHOR

Aurelia writes contemporary romance and enjoys reading it just as much! She lives in Alabama with her husband, daughter, and fur babies. She spends most of her time caring for her loved ones and plotting stories. She's excited to share her stories and to grow as an author. Look for more outstanding stories from Aurelia by following her on social media.

Made in the USA
Columbia, SC
19 July 2023